The Story of Mousey Brown

Written by James Glenn

Illustrations by Molly Rowbotham

I originally wrote this story for my little brother Stan in 2010 for World Book Day, as he hadn't done his homework and chosen a book.

Proudly proclaiming
his big brother would write one for him.

This is that book.

As the soft morning sun rose over Rodent Town, there woke up a young mouse called Mousey Brown

Now, this young mouse was unlike the rest.
All the grown up mice thought of
even him as a pest!

He would play jokes on the adults,
and hide their cheese in the hay.
He wouldn't share his blueberries
All until just one day...

and on this
one day,

old Grey Mouse
had enough, he
said

'You better calm
down Brown!

or else I'm gonna
get rough!'

Young Master Brown just
laughed in his face, he teased
'An old mouse like you?
putting ME in my place!?!'

Its safe to
say old Grey
mouse was
not best
pleased

especially
since
Mousey
Brown had
eaten all of
his cheese!

KEYWORD	DEFINITION
THYROID-STIMULATING HORMONE	A pituitary hormone that stimulates the thyroid gland to secrete the hormone thyroxine.
THYROXINE	A hormone made and released by the thyroid gland and required for normal growth and body metabolism.
TISSUE	A collection of similar cells that perform a specific task.
TISSUE CULTURE	The growing of plant and animal cells in the laboratory on or in special culture media.
TISSUE FLUID	A liquid formed when plasma is filtered through capillaries into the surrounding spaces. It has no cellular components but many substances such as glucose and amino acids in solution.
TISSUE TYPING	Mapping of the antigens on cell surfaces. An important tool used in transplantations, where matching of tissue types is critical to the success of the procedure.
TOXIN	A chemical product of an organism, such as a bacterium, which is harmful to other living things.
TRACHEID	A long, slender cell that is part of the xylem. A tracheid has no living contents and its wall contains lignin for added strength.
TRANSCRIPTION	The formation of messenger ribonucleic acid (mRNA) from deoxyribonucleic acid (DNA) in the nucleus. Transcription requires the enzyme RNA polymerase to be present.
TRANSFER RIBONUCLEIC ACID	A variety of RNA that carries specific amino acids to the ribosomes during the translation process.
TRANSGENIC	An organism that has been modified by having genetic material from an unrelated organism inserted into its chromosomes.
TRANSLATION	Conversion of the information on the transcribed messenger ribonucleic acid (mRNA) molecule into a sequence of amino acids in the nucleus by ribosomes.
TRANSLOCATION	The movement of dissolved materials in a plant which involves the movement of sugar through phloem.
TRANSLOCATION MUTATION	A change in the genetic material whereby a piece of a chromosome has been broken off and then has attached itself to another chromosome.
TRANSMITTED LIGHT	Light that passes straight through a surface without being absorbed.

So he spent the whole morning conducting a scheme

that would show young Brown what the other mice mean.

So he gathered the town
and told them the score
and that Mr Brown would be changed,
of that he was sure!

As Mousey Brown, all alone,
played in the grass
all the other mice would leave
Rodent Town on mass!

When the young mouse got back from his play he called for his mother but it seemed she was away.

Now young Brown was puzzled
but he was sure that his mother
must of just popped next door.

But when he
went over,
he was very
surprised

the whole of
Rodent Town
had
disappeared
before his
eyes.

He searched up
in the steeple

and down in the park

even in the Mouse
Trap Inn basement
where it was scary and dark

As young Mousey Brown sat alone in
Rodent Town square

a tear fell from his whisker
'didn't the other mice care?

They've left
me to fend for
myself all
alone!

Now I'm all by
myself in my
Rodent Town
home!'

he cried and he cried

and then he
cried some more

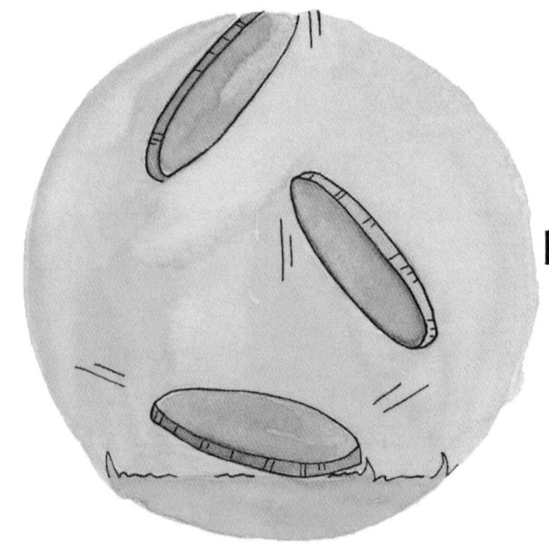

then suddenly the
penny dropped to the floor

'I have done this,
I've drove them away!'
'I didn't want them to
hate me,
I just wanted to play!'

and with his
revelation
appeared old
mouse Grey

'I'm sorry Mr
Grey!'

said young
Mousey
Brown

'Ill give you
MY cheese
back!'

'calm yourself down young little mouse do you know why we left you all alone in the house?'

'is it because I am nasty?' replied Brown 'well sort of' said Mr Gray 'we wanted to show you what might happen someday

if you treat all your friends like
you don't even care
then one day you might find,
that they're not even there!'

So young Mousey Brown wiped
the tears of his whiskers
and apologised for being
so rude and malicious

he promised that he would never do it again
and from now on
he would play normal mouse games.

Like paw ball
or mouse conkers,
which is like normal conkers
but with pepper corns.

THE END...

Stay tuned for more stories
from Rodent Town!

Printed in Great Britain
by Amazon